This b

I celebrated World Book Day 2017

with this brilliant gift from my local Bookseller,

&

JUDI CURTIN

This book has been specially written and published to celebrate
20 years of World Book Day. For further information, visit
www.worldbookday.com.

World Book Day in the UK and Ireland is made possible by
generous sponsorship from National Book Tokens, participating
publishers, authors, illustrators and booksellers.

Booksellers who accept the £1* World Book Day Book Token
bear the full cost of redeeming it.

World Book Day, World Book Night and Quick Reads are annual initiatives designed to encourage everyone in the UK and Ireland — whatever your age — to read more and discover the joy of books and reading for pleasure.

World Book Night is a celebration of books and reading for adults and teens on 23 April, which sees book gifting and celebrations in thousands of communities around the country: www.worldbooknight.org

Quick Reads provides brilliant short new books by bestselling authors to engage adults in reading: www.quickreads.org.uk

*€1.50 in Ireland

First published 2017 by The O'Brien Press Ltd.,
12 Terenure Road East, Rathgar, Dublin 6, D06 HD27, Ireland.
Tel: +353 1 4923333; Fax: +353 1 4922777
E-mail: books@obrien.ie
Website: www.obrien.ie
The O'Brien Press is a member of Publishing Ireland.

ISBN: 978-1-84717-889-3

1 3 5 7 9 10 8 6 4 2

17 19 20 18

Layout and design: The O'Brien Press Ltd.

Printed and bound by CPI Group (UK) Ltd, Croydon, CR0 4YY

The paper used in this book is produced using pulp from managed forests.

Published in

DUBLIN
UNESCO
City of Literature

Judi Curtin

Fast Forward

THE O'BRIEN PRESS
DUBLIN

JUDI CURTIN grew up in Cork and now lives in Limerick, where she is married with three children. Judi is the author of the first book about Molly and Beth, *Time After Time*, as well as the best-selling 'Eva' and 'Alice & Megan' series. With Roisin Meaney, she is the author of *See If I Care*. Her books have been published in German, Portuguese, Finnish, Swedish, Norwegian, Russian, Serbian and Turkish, and in Australia and New Zealand.

Other Books by Judi Curtin

Time After Time

The 'Alice & Megan' series

Alice Next Door
Alice Again
Don't Ask Alice
Alice in the Middle
Bonjour Alice
Alice & Megan Forever
Alice to the Rescue
Viva Alice!
Alice & Megan's Cookbook

The 'Eva' Series

Eva's Journey
Eva's Holiday
Leave it to Eva
Eva and the Hidden Diary
Only Eva

See If I Care (with Roisín Meaney)

Chapter One

'We're invited to a party.'

'Yay! Whose party? When is it? What are we going to wear?'

Beth gave me her phone so I could read the text.

Hey Beth, it's Heather. Maybe you and your sister would like to come to my birthday party on Sunday? It's in Fernando's at 4 o' clock. Let me know if you can't make it – but I hope you can! xxx

For a second I wasn't even sure who Heather was, and then I remembered the new girl who'd shown up in our class two weeks earlier – and I understood why Beth wasn't excited about the party.

'It's from Heather,' I said.

'Top marks for stating the obvious.'

I tried to whack Beth with my pillow – but after years of practice she's good at ducking.

'So I'm guessing you don't want to go?'

Beth thought for a bit before answering. 'I don't think so. I mean Heather's probably lovely and everything, but she's so .... quiet.'

'I know. She must be the quietest girl in the history of the world. She was in our class for a whole week before I knew she could actually talk.'

'Remember when the teacher asked her a question yesterday, her face nearly turned purple, like talking to a teacher is the most embarrassing thing ever? I even got embarrassed watching her.'

'Me too – and I was sitting at the other side of the room.'

'And it's not like she's our best friend or anything,' said Beth. 'We hardly know the girl.'

'So how come she's got your number?'

'She asked me for it after choir practice the other day. I thought it was a bit weird, since we'd never talked before – but she was all red-faced and shy so I couldn't say no.'

'That's not a bit weird, it's totally weird,' I said. 'Who asks randomers for their phone number?'

'Weird kids?'

I giggled. 'Parties are meant to be fun, but I'm not sure about this one. I don't know what I'd even say to Heather for more than five seconds – she's so quiet and awkward.'

'Exactly.'

'Did she ask for anyone else's number?'

'Yes,' said Beth. 'She asked all the girls in the choir – kind of brave of her, I guess, since she's so shy.'

'That's great news.'

'It is?'

'Yeah, I bet Heather's asked *all* the choir girls to her party – so she won't care if you and me are there or not.'

'True – and my dad promised to take us to the movies on Sunday, remember?'

'That's settled then – we won't go. Will you text Heather and let her know?'

A minute later Beth handed me her phone.

'Does this sound OK?' she asked as I read

the words on the screen.

Hey Heather, Thanks for asking us to your party but we've already got plans for Sunday afternoon – sorry bout that. Hope it's great anyway. PS Molly's not my sister – we just live together.

'Perfect,' I said. 'Send that and then we can get on with our lives.'

But before she could send the message, Beth stamped across the room and plugged her phone into the charger.

'My stupid phone's died again!' she said. 'The battery only lasts for about two and a half minutes. I'm so totally fed up of it.'

'And your dad hasn't changed his mind about buying you a new phone?'

She shook her head. 'It's like he's living in the dark ages. He says I should just put up with it and spend more time playing out-side.'

'You could save up and buy a new one?'

'Have you actually seen how much pocket money I get? I'd be saving for hundreds of years. I wish there was an easy way of get-ting money. I wish ……….. OMG, Molly. I've just had the most amazing idea.'

'What?'

'Wait and see! Now put on your shoes – we're going out.'

* * *

'What do you see?' asked Beth.

'Well, duh. We're looking in the window of a phone shop, so I see lots of phones. Only problem is, you can't afford any of them. You can hardly afford the fake ones for babies that they sell in the euro store.'

'Very funny! Except I'm not looking at the phones. I'm looking over there.'

She was pointing at a big round jar on a shelf behind the counter of the shop. The jar was filled to the top with old sim cards, and on the label it said – 'Guess How Many'.

On the wall behind the counter there was a big poster:

Guess the exact number of cards in the jar and win your choice of phone.

New competition every month.

ONLY TWO EURO PER ENTRY!

(Draw takes place at 3pm on the last day of every month)

'But my mum's talked to us about that,' I said. 'She says it's a complete scam.'

'Yeah, but–'

'Don't even think about it. Mum watched them counting out the sim cards last month. She said it was totally mean – one poor man came really, really close, but because he was out by a few he got nothing – and the phone shop owner got a big heap of euros. It *so* wasn't fair.'

'Yeah, but how about if we sort of – made the odds go more in our favour?'

'You mean by buying loads of tickets? But you can't afford that, and even if you could–'

'I'm not buying loads of tickets,' said Beth. 'I've got a *much* better plan than that.'

'Like what?'

'Just follow me and all will be revealed.'

Chapter Two

a few minutes later, Beth led me down a stinky old alleyway – and I got the first clue of what was going on in her head.

'No way,' I said. 'That's never going to work – and even if it did ...'

She grinned. 'It's worth a try, isn't it?'

By now we were standing under a faded old sign that said 'Rico's Store'. Even thinking about our last visit made me feel shaky and weak.

Beth hugged me. 'I know it was scary the last time – but it all worked out in the end, didn't it?'

'Yeah, but time travel freaks me out – and

how exactly is it going to help you to win a phone anyway?'

(I'm not a complete idiot. By now I had a fair idea of what Beth was thinking, but I wanted to hear her say the words, just to be sure.)

'We go forward to the end of the month – that's this Sunday – and we watch phone-shop woman counting out the sim cards. Then all we have to do is remember the number, come back to now, and enter the competition. Easy-peasy.'

'It's totally not easy. If we go through Rico's creepy door, how do we know we'll end up where we want to be? We could end up in the past – or hundreds of years in the future.'

'That'd be kind of cool. We could….'

Beth's usually fairly sensible, but when it comes to time travel, it's like she forgets who she's supposed to be.

'I'm serious,' I said. 'How do we know ...?'

'Well last time, I really wanted to see my mum, and that's what happened, so I'm guessing if we concentrate really hard on the last day of the month, we'll end up there.'

'And let's pretend for a minute that this crazy plan works out,' I said. 'Is it right?'

'What do you mean?'

'Well, it's kind of cheating, isn't it?'

'Weeeell, maybe sort of – but no point arguing about that now. You say it won't work anyway, so why don't we just see what happens? Now, are you coming or not?'

'I'm really not sure about......'

But Beth was already opening the door

and I didn't want to miss out on a cool adventure, so I crossed my fingers and followed her in to Rico's Store.

* * *

Rico was polishing a sparkly blue bottle, just like before.

He looked up.

'Hello, girls. So nice to see you again.'

Again?

Now I was seriously freaked out.

How come he remembered us?

How come his eyes were so weird?

How come Beth was smiling at him, instead of racing back out the door?

'So how can I help you this time?'

He sounded all concerned and helpful, but that didn't make me feel any better.

I had a horrible feeling that Rico wasn't

going to be a big fan of Beth's phone-winning plan.

Maybe he put shrinking spells on people he didn't like?

Maybe all those creepy bottles on the shelves were full of tiny, trapped people who'd tried to do bad stuff like cheating in competitions?

Maybe hundreds of little fists were beating on glass, trying to get our attention, begging us to save them?

Was there someone in that sparkly blue bottle?

But Beth just smiled. 'Oh, Molly and I weren't doing much today so we thought we'd like to go on an adventure,' she said. 'Would you mind if we …?'

Rico pointed to the black curtain behind

him. 'Be my guests,' he said.

I sooo didn't want to be his guest, but Beth was already headed for the curtain, and just like the last time, I followed her.

Chapter Three

This time everything happened at top speed. There was the silence, the thick, warm darkness, the cinnamon smell, and then the sudden flash of bright light and the sound of a door closing softly.

Before my eyes had time to recover, Beth grabbed my arm.

'OMG, Molly. It worked. It totally worked.'

I slowly opened my eyes. Behind us was a door saying *Rico's Store – Emergency Entrance.*

'This is crazy,' I said. 'Let's go back, Beth. Remember this door vanished on us before and I so don't want–'

'No way. We're not going back. Look over there.'

It seemed impossible, but we were standing a few doors away from the phone shop. Beth looked happy, but I was suspicious – it all seemed much too easy.

'Hang on a sec,' I said. 'Maybe it's a trick.'

'What do you mean? We're definitely in the right place.'

'I get that – but maybe we're not in the right *time*. Maybe Rico was too clever for us. Maybe it's still today – or maybe it's last week, or last year. We could go back through the emergency entrance and find Rico rolling on the floor laughing at us.'

Beth looked worried for a second, but then she turned to a little kid walking past.

'Hey,' she said. 'What's the date?'

'Little kids never know ...' I began, but the boy grinned at us, showing us a big gap where his two front teeth should be. 'It's the 30th,' he said. 'It's my birthday and I'm a big seven and now I'm allowed to walk all the way to the shop on my own.'

'Happy birthday,' said Beth.

I still didn't want to give up.

'Maybe it's evening time,' I said. 'Maybe the draw was on hours ago. Maybe the shop is locked up and everyone's gone home for their tea.'

Maybe we can forget this whole thing.

Beth pointed to the clock tower at the end of the street.

'Five to three,' she said. 'Good old Rico, he got us here just in time.'

'But ...'

'But what?'

What could I say? Beth was right. We really had jumped forward in time. Only seconds had passed, but Beth and I were two days older. In real life, the boy in front of us should still be six. It should be Friday and Beth and I should be at home fighting over whose turn it was to set the table for dinner.

'But nothing,' I said.

'Well let's get going. We don't want to miss the big count.'

* * *

The shop was crowded, but Beth grabbed my arm and we wriggled our way to the front, right next to the counter.

The phone-shop woman was opening the

sim-card jar. On the wall next to her was a big chart with people's names and the numbers they had guessed.

'OMG,' whispered Beth. 'It looks like there's more than a hundred names there – someone *has* to get the right number.'

'Maybe not,' I said. 'Mum said the competition's been running for months and months and no one's ever won.'

'Something tells me I've got it right this time,' said a boy next to me. 'I'm so excited I think I'm going to pee myself.'

That so would not be funny. I edged away as much as I could in the crowded space. The boy looked nice, and I felt sorry for him. It would be a miracle if he, or anyone else, got the right number – and I was guessing Beth was the only one who actually had magic to help her.

'I know exactly which phone I'm going to pick,' said the boy. 'If I can walk out of here with that phone in my hand, I'll be the happiest boy in the whole wide world.'

I felt sick.

* * *

The phone-shop woman took the first sim-card out of the jar and held it in the air. 'One,' she said, before dropping it into a box on the counter.

'Two,' she said, as she slowly held up the second sim card.

'Get on with it,' called a woman from the back. 'I've got shopping to do.'

After that the counting went a bit quicker. All around us, people seemed tense and nervous. The boy next to me was jigging up and down, like the floor was too hot for his feet.

When the count came to 194, a woman near us gave a big sigh. 'That's me gone for another month,' she said, as she pushed her way towards the door.

Gradually more and more people realised they hadn't won and they left. None of them looked very happy – and I couldn't blame them.

I wanted the whole thing to be over. I didn't want to be part of Beth's phone-winning plan. I wanted the nice boy next to us to win, so he could get a phone without cheating, and Beth and I could get on with our real lives.

The sim-card jar was nearly empty, and the boy was going crazy. 'I'm close,' he said.

'I'm really, really close. All I need is for there to be twenty more sim cards in that jar – and the phone I've been dreaming of will be mine.'

The poor kid – I couldn't blame him for hoping but it was easy to see that there were only five or six more sim cards to go.

I felt sick as the seconds ticked by and I watched his hopes fade away. When the phone-shop woman pulled the last sim-card from the jar, the boy stopped jigging around. He went quiet and pale.

'I was only a little bit out.' His voice was a whisper. 'I've never been so close before.'

'I'm so sorry,' I said. 'I wish you had won. I really do. Maybe next–'

But I couldn't finish my sentence

because Beth grabbed my arm and pulled
me out of the shop.

Chapter Four

'What?' I said when we were safely at the other end of the street. 'Why couldn't we stay to see if someone won the prize?'

'Because, for one thing, no one looked happy so I'm guessing that's because nobody won, and ...'

'And what?'

'Well, if I actually saw someone winning, I don't think I could go through with this whole thing. If I came along tomorrow or yesterday or whatever it is, and guessed the same number, we might only get half a phone each – and that wouldn't be fair.'

'And otherwise it *would* be fair?'

'Well, the phone shop's cheating everyone. They should give the prize to the person who comes closest to the number of sim cards, but they don't. They've fixed it so chances are no one will ever win.'

'That's not really the point,' I said. 'Look at it like this, Beth. Imagine we're back here, and you've "guessed" the right number. You're standing in front of all the people who've never really had a chance of winning, and they're clapping and cheering, and they're happy for you. How do you feel?'

'Over the moon because I've just won a totally cool phone?'

'Seriously?'

Beth didn't answer, so I knew she was starting to agree with me.

'Beth?'

'You're right, Molly,' she said. 'I'd feel awful if I won. I couldn't bear to have all those people staring at me, happy that I'd won, and not knowing that I'd cheated. Now that I've been here, I understand that this whole thing was a bad idea. I really, really want a new phone, but getting one like that, well that's not really worth it.'

I hugged her. 'That's what I think too.'

'So I guess we should go back home now?'

'Why don't we hang out here for a bit?'

'And do what?'

'Maybe we can meet our future selves. We can see how old and wise we're going to be in two days time. I want to see if this gross spot on my chin will be gone.'

'Meeting ourselves would be super weird,'

said Beth. 'And it could be dangerous. Maybe we'd evaporate or explode or something.'

'Well, chances are we won't meet ourselves, but we can still walk around and see if anything's changed.'

She giggled. 'It's only been two days, but why not? Let's go on an adventure.'

Chapter Five

'**B**eth?'

'What?'

'Is it just me, or is walking around the future just as boring as walking around the present?'

'Totally. Let's go back. We can ... oh look, we're nearly at Fernandos!'

'And?'

'It's Sunday afternoon, remember? Heather's party will be on. We can peep in and see what we're missing.'

* * *

The window was high up, so Beth dragged a stool from the terrace.

'Be careful,' I whispered, as she climbed up. 'Don't let Heather see you – we're supposed to have plans this afternoon – and I don't think spying on her party counts as a plan.'

'I'm *being* careful.'

'And the window's open too, so don't let her hear you either.'

'Do I look like an idiot?'

She leaned her elbows on the windowsill and peeped in.

'What can you see?' I whispered. 'Are there tons of people there? Does it look like they're having fun? What's Heather wearing?'

Beth didn't answer.

'Hey,' I said. 'If there's something amazing going on, I want to see it too.'

Beth climbed down from the stool. 'It's not amazing,' she said. 'It's totally not amazing. Oh, Molly, we've been so mean!'

I had no idea what she was on about, so I climbed up to see for myself. The restaurant wasn't very big, and it was easy to see Heather sitting at a big table just near the window. The table was set for loads of people, but the only ones there were Heather, her mum and dad, and a cross-looking boy who I guessed had to be her big brother.

Heather's mum and dad were chatting to her and smiling, but she didn't look very happy.

I know eavesdropping is really bad, but I had to know what they were saying, so I leaned in closer.

'Did everyone text to say they couldn't

come?' asked Heather's dad.

She shook her head. 'Some did, but a few didn't answer, so I thought ...'

'Don't worry, darling,' said her mum. 'Maybe everyone's got delayed.'

'It's nearly five o'clock. No one's coming. Face it, Mum, those kids in my old school were right – your daughter's a loser.'

Her brother laughed, and for a second I felt like running into the restaurant and punching his face.

Couldn't he see how upset Heather was?

She was trying to be brave, but her eyes were all shiny with tears. Her dad put his arm around her, but I could see that wasn't helping a whole lot. The poor girl hadn't done anything wrong, but still she looked sad and ashamed.

I climbed slowly down from the stool.

'This is the worst thing we've ever, ever done,' I said. 'Would it have been so hard for us to be nice and go to Heather's party?'

'It seemed hard at the time, but now … OMG! I've just remembered something.'

'What?'

'We haven't actually done the bad thing yet. Remember my phone died before I could send the text?'

'Yeah, but …'

'Think about it Molly.'

'I *am* thinking about it – and it's making my head hurt.'

'We have no idea how this time travel thing really works.'

'That's for sure.'

'Maybe what we just saw is the future that

might have been. Maybe things will turn out differently if we go back home and text Heather and say we'll go to her party.'

'But what about the movies?'

'Dad can take us to the movies another time. This is much more important.'

'So why are we hanging around here? Let's head back and see if we can fix this mess.'

* * *

Rico was still polishing the sparkly blue bottle.

Is that what he did all day long, every single day?

Was this his punishment for something bad he did millions of years ago?

'Welcome back, girls,' he said. 'Did you get what you wanted?'

Well, we were trying to go into the future to win a phone by cheating, but instead we discovered that we'd sort of accidentally done a really mean and cruel thing, so now we're in a hurry to go and fix it.

I didn't fancy saying that to anyone, and especially not to a weird guy like Rico, so I didn't answer his question.

'Er, we're going home now,' I said.

'We've got important stuff to do,' said Beth, as we headed for the door.

'There's just one thing,' said Rico, making us both stop suddenly. 'Using the back entrance is a privilege – it's not offered to everyone, you know.'

'Oh,' I said. 'Thanks very much for letting us use it.'

He stepped in front of us. 'And with

privilege comes responsibility. Do you understand?'

What I understood was that this guy seemed to be able to read our minds.

Did he know all about our plan to win the phone?

Should Beth and I admit what we had nearly done?

Or would that make things even worse?

'Er, we totally get all that privilege and responsibility stuff,' said Beth. 'And, being honest, I *was* thinking about doing a bad thing, but I'm not going to do it now.'

'I'm delighted to hear it,' said Rico, who didn't look very delighted. 'Maybe the power protected you from yourself.'

I had no idea what he was on about, and I didn't fancy hanging around to find out.

Rico stared at us for a second, and then he stepped out of the way, and Beth and I raced out of the shop.

* * *

Hi Heather,

Thanks so much for inviting us to your party. It sounds really great, and Molly and I would love to go. See you there!

(PS Molly's not my sister. We just live together.)

'What do you think?' asked Beth. 'Is that OK?'

'Perfect.'

Beth sent the message and then she kept on typing.

'What are you doing?' I asked.

'I'm texting all the girls in the choir, saying we're going to the party and that I think they should go too.'

'Brilliant,' I said. 'Let's make sure that Heather has the best birthday ever.'

Chapter Six

'**H**eather's going to totally love those earrings you got her,' I said as we walked home from our shopping trip the next day.

'And she's going to *adore* the bracelet you chose,' said Beth.

'I'm actually looking forward to the party now. It could be ...'

'Why have you stopped talking?' asked Beth. 'Have your batteries run out?'

'Look,' I said. 'It's him.'

'It's who?'

'It's the boy from the phone-shop. The one who was standing next to me when they were counting out the sim cards. You probably didn't notice him because you were so busy trying to win the phone. He was so upset when he didn't win. It sounded like he'd been entering the competition for months.'

Before I could say any more, he was right next to us.

'Hey,' I said.

He looked up. 'Er ... hey,' he said as he kept on walking.

'I can see you made a big impression on him too,' said Beth, giggling.

'How come he has *no* idea who I am?' I said, not sure if I should feel insulted or angry. 'It's only a few days since ......'

And then I remembered.

'It's not me,' I said. 'It's him.'

'What do you mean?'

'He can't remember me because we haven't met yet. It's still only Saturday, and we don't get to meet him until tomorrow, remember?

'It's so weird that we're having this conversation. I'm not sure if ......'

'OMG! Hold that thought. I've just had the most amazing idea.'

* * *

I quickly told Beth what I was thinking.

'That's such a cool idea,' she said. 'But it's not going to work if we stand here like idiots – we can't let him get away.'

And so Beth and I followed the boy for a bit. I guess we were acting like two crazy stalkers, but it took a while for me to get up the courage to do what I wanted to do.

'Hey,' I called in the end, and he stopped

walking and turned around.

'I'm sorry,' he said. 'But do I know you?'

'Yes ... no ... not exactly,' I said. 'It's the weirdest thing, and I can't explain it properly but ...'

I didn't finish the sentence, partly because I didn't know how, and partly because he was looking at me like I was an idiot.

Beth decided to save me.

'Is this the way to the phone-shop?' she asked.

'Actually it is,' he said. 'I'm on my way there now.'

'Buying a new phone?' asked Beth, nudging me.

'No,' he said. 'I wish I could afford one.'

'So why are you going to the phone shop?'

He didn't seem to mind that Beth was

being so nosy.

'I'm going because they run this competition every month.'

He went on to explain about the competition. Of course we knew about it already, and it was hard to pay attention anyway, because of the way Beth was poking me in the ribs with her very sharp finger.

'OMG,' said Beth then. 'This is the weirdest thing.'

'What?' he asked politely.

'I've just remembered this crazy dream I had last night.'

He didn't say anything – the poor boy probably thought *he* was having a crazy dream right now.

'In my dream,' continued Beth. 'There was a competition to guess a number – it's so weird, it has to be a sign of something.'

A sign that you're losing your marbles?

'You should guess the number I dreamed of, and I bet you'll win the phone.'

'If it's that easy, why don't you enter the competition?' he asked.

'That's a very good point,' I said. 'Except Beth and I – our families come from ....'

'From where?' he asked.

'Er ... from a country very far away from here ... and where we come from ... we're not allowed to enter competitions.'

I knew it was lame, and Beth rolled her eyes to show me she felt the same.

'So that's why we want to help you,' she said. 'If you use the number I dreamed of, I bet you'll win.'

Suddenly the boy smiled – but it was the

kind of smile you give to a little kid when they've told you about their imaginary friend, or the magic sword they keep under their bed. He didn't believe a single word we were saying – and nothing was going to change his mind.

'Forget it,' I said. 'We were just kidding around, weren't we, Beth?'

'We were?'

'Yes,' I said. 'Oh, and maybe you shouldn't enter the competition anyway. It's not really fair.'

Now the poor guy looked totally confused. 'Er, I need to go,' he said. 'Bye.'

As soon as he was far enough away, Beth and I fell around laughing.

'OMG,' I said. 'We totally messed with his head – the poor boy thinks we're totally crazy.'

'Maybe we are,' she said. 'Maybe we are.'

Chapter Seven

'Going to a party?'

It was Nadzia, a girl we knew from the soccer club. She was pointing at the beautifully wrapped presents Beth and I were carrying.

'Yeah,' said Beth. 'There's a new girl in our class, Heather, and it's her birthday today. A lot of us are going to her party.'

'Is that Heather Dempsey?' asked Nadzia.

I had no idea what Heather's second name was, but Beth nodded.

'That's her,' she said. 'Do you know her?'

'Sort of – she used to be in the class below me at school. How's she doing these days?'

'I have no idea,' said Beth. 'She's really, really quiet.'

'I guess it's hard to blame her,' said Nadzia. 'After what happened last year.'

'What happened last year?' I asked.

'It was awful. This new girl, Teegan, came to her class. She was very pretty and funny and had amazing cool clothes. Nearly everyone wanted to be friends with her.'

'I'm not seeing the problem here,' I said.

'Well,' said Nadzia. 'The problem is, Teegan was as mean as a snake. You know the kind of girl who's all smiley to your face, and then when you turn your back she starts saying mean stuff about you.'

'Ouch,' said Beth.

'And it gets worse,' said Nadzia. 'Just because Heather wasn't fooled by Teegan's fake sweetness, Teegan started to be really, really horrible to her.'

'What did she do?' I asked.

'Loads of stuff. She made up bad stories about Heather – and she's a really good liar, so loads of the kids believed her. And whenever Heather said something in class, they'd all giggle and whisper about her.'

Now I felt sick. No wonder the poor girl didn't like talking in class.

'Heather used to be really confident before,' said Nadzia. 'And at first she tried to defend herself, but in the end ... I guess no one wants to be the girl everyone laughs at.'

'And what about Heather's friends?' asked Beth. 'Didn't they stand up for her?'

'Some of them did – at first,' said Nadzia. 'But then ... I don't know if they were afraid of Teegan or dazzled by her but ... whatever happened, they weren't there for Heather when she needed them.'

'That's so awful,' I said.

'It is – and I guess you can see why Heather decided to change schools. Anyway, it looks like she's lucked out now.'

'What do you mean?' asked Beth.

'Well you two are going to her party, and you said lots of others are too,' said Nadzia. 'Heather's really cool, and if people are nice to her, I'm sure she'll get her confidence back soon. Anyway, I gotta go. See you at practice next week.'

'OMG, Beth,' I said as Nadzia walked away. 'I think we owe Rico a bunch of flowers or a new polishing-cloth or something. He stopped us from making the biggest mistake in the history of the world.'

* * *

Beth and I were the first guests to arrive at the party.

'Look,' said Beth, pointing to where Heather was sitting with her parents and brother. 'They're over there.'

'I know,' I said. 'I've been here before, remember?'

'I'm trying not to think about that,' said Beth. 'It's all too weird.'

When Heather saw us she gave a huge big smile, like us being there was the best thing that had ever, ever happened to her. When she opened her presents, and saw the bracelet and earrings, she practically jumped up and down.

'I love them,' she said, as she hugged us. 'I

totally, totally love them.'

I was glad she liked our presents, but even more glad that suddenly Heather didn't seem shy or awkward. She just seemed like an ordinary, happy kid, as she ran over to welcome the next two guests.

* * *

'That was so much fun,' said Beth as we walked out of Fernando's later. 'Heather's mum and dad are really nice, and her brother's not too bad – maybe teasing is what big brothers are supposed to do.'

'Yeah, and when someone mentioned bullying, it was totally cute the way he put his arm around Heather and changed the subject.'

'Yeah,' I said. 'Heather's so nice and I'm glad you asked her over to our place after school tomorrow. I really hope we can make her forget she ever met that awful Teegan.'

'OMG,' said Beth. 'How about we go back in time and play a really mean trick on Teegan? We could ......'

'I've done enough time travelling for this weekend,' I said. 'How about we go home and see if we can persuade your dad to bring us to the late movie show?'

'Excellent idea.'

Then my friend put her arm around me and we set off for home.

If you loved Fast Forward, you'll enjoy

The first book in the Star Club series

by Natasha Mac'aBháird

Turn the page for a sneak peek …

Chapter One

It's impossible to get any peace in my house.

Either Zach and Bobby are chasing each other (or Maisie) around the house, or they're playing football on the landing and using my bedroom door as the goal. Or else it's Maisie taking over the sitting room with all her dolls and teddies, or Emma crawling along and wrecking Maisie's game. And then Maisie crying and having to be comforted, and Emma either laughing or else joining in and crying too.

I share a room with Maisie, so I can't even escape up there for a bit of quiet, because she's sure to come in and out getting more teddies, or wanting me to play with her. I have been BEGGING Mum to change things around so I can have my own bedroom, but so far the most she has said is 'we'll see'. Which is better than an outright 'no', but not by much.

I said it to Mum. I said, 'It's impossible to get any peace in this house.'

Well, you would swear I had just made the best joke in the history of the earth. She practically fell off her chair laughing.

'What's so funny?' I demanded.

When she finally stopped laughing enough to answer me, all she would say was, 'I've been saying the same thing for years.'

Which wasn't much help to me.

So there I was, the poor unfortunate

eldest child, with four younger siblings caus-
ing endless chaos, and one unsympathetic
mother who could only laugh at me. The
summer holidays were stretching out before
me, long and empty and very, very noisy.

I really wished I was going to drama camp
with Isabel, a girl in my class. She'd been
telling me all about it and it sounded amazing. The kids were going to write their own
show and then at the end of the two weeks
they'd put it on for their parents. Lucky
Isabel – it sounded like so much fun. I would
have loved every minute.

I didn't even ask Mum if I could go
because it wouldn't have been fair. The camp
was so far away – at least half an hour's drive.
I couldn't ask Mum to load all the kids into
the car and drive me there every morning,

and then do the same again to collect me. Anyway, I'd feel a bit like I was abandoning her. Dad works long hours, and since Emma came along Mum has been relying on me a lot to help out. Even though Zach's only three years younger than me he's a bit of a daydreamer – he's got his head in the clouds most of the time. If you ask him to help with something he will, but I just do stuff without being asked. My brothers think I'm bossy, but actually I'm just pretty organised.

What I needed was a project. Not a school project, obviously. I'm not that crazy. The best thing about the summer is having a very long break from schoolwork of any kind. But I'm the sort of person who always likes to be doing something. I like to have a plan to focus on and to feel like I'm achieving something. I just needed to work out what that something should be.

The day before, I'd spent most of the afternoon playing teddies with Maisie. If I didn't find something to do quickly, I'd be sucked into another game. It wouldn't be so bad if I could call for Ruby, but she was at ballet camp that morning.

As if she knew what I was thinking, Mum said, 'Why don't you call for Ruby?'

'I can't, she's got ballet camp,' I reminded her. 'She's not going to be home until lunchtime.'

'Oh, that's a pity.'

I knew what was coming next. I just knew it.

'Why don't you call for the girl next door then?' Mum went on. 'She seemed really friendly.'

I'm not sure how Mum had worked THAT one out. The day before, we'd seen some new people moving in next door – a mum and a girl about my age. Mum kept saying she should go over and introduce herself, but something kept getting in the way, so all she had managed to do was say 'hello' as she rushed to pick Maisie up after she fell off her bike. They were unpacking lots of bags from their car at the time, and looked pretty busy themselves, so I don't really know how Mum could have somehow decided that the girl was really friendly. She might be lovely, sure. She might also be boring, or weird, or mean. It was a bit hard to tell from one 'hi'. But trust Mum to think that just because we lived next door to each other we were bound to end up as best buddies.

'She said hello, that's all. And only after you'd said it to her first.'

'Well, I thought she seemed nice,' Mum said. 'Anyway, why don't you call for her and find out?'

'I don't know, Mum. It's not like I'm Maisie's age where you can just go and play with anyone.' It was an important point, I thought. At twelve, you're a bit more discerning about who you hang around with.

'Come on, Hannah, it's the nice thing to do. She probably doesn't know anyone here yet. Why don't you see if she wants to go rollerblading?'

I could see Mum wasn't going to let the subject drop. And now that she'd played the 'nice thing to do' card I was stuck. 'Oh, all right then! But can you come and call me after half an hour? Then I have an excuse to leave if I've had enough.'

Mum laughed. 'No problem. I'll be sure to pop out in between feeding Emma and hanging out my third load of washing.'

'Hey, it's the least you can do after making me go off with a complete stranger,' I told her.

'You know what they say, Hannah. A stranger is a friend you haven't yet met!'

A stranger is a friend you haven't yet met? Yeah, right! Only the other day she was warning me about not talking to strangers, and never getting into a car with someone you don't know, even if they say they just want you to show them something on a map, and never going off with someone even if they ask you to help them find their lost cat.

Although, to be fair, the girl next door didn't exactly look like the kind of stranger who would bundle you into a car and kidnap you. But you never know.

I went to the cupboard under the stairs to look for my rollerblades. Not an easy job, considering it's the place where all seven members of my family dump everything that doesn't have a home. (Well, I guess Emma doesn't, but that's because she's only eight months old. There's still stuff belonging to her in there, or things that used to belong to Maisie and that Mum is waiting for Emma to grow into.) Sometimes when we're having people over Mum runs around the house with a laundry basket and picks up all the clutter and shoves the whole lot under the stairs to deal with later. I've lost many pieces of valuable artwork that way; Mum just says that it's my own fault for leaving it lying around.

I opened the door very carefully, because you really never know what's going to land on top of you. Luckily I spotted my rollerblades right away, tucked under Zach's old tricycle and a pile of newspapers Dad claimed he was going to get around to reading at the weekend. I hauled them out, managing not to dislodge the entire mound of things around it. It took me another few minutes to find my helmet and knee and elbow pads, which Mum won't let me skate without, even though I pretty much never fall over.

'Hannah, are you coming to play teddies?'

Maisie demanded. She was standing behind me, and as I turned all I could see was the top of her hair above her armful of stuffed toys.

'Not right now,' I told her.

'Oh, please, Hannah?' A blue rabbit fell out of the pile, revealing a sad little face.

I felt bad, but I needed some twelve-year-old company, even if it was the stranger next door. 'Sorry, Maisie. I'm going out roller-blading. Maybe later, OK?'

I picked up the rollerblades and headed for the door, ignoring Maisie's protests. 'Bye, Mum!' I called.

Once I was outside though, I suddenly found myself feeling a bit shy. If you knew me you'd realise this is unusual. I'm sort of a leader in my little group of friends. I think it comes from being the oldest of a big family. You just have to be ready to take charge if you want anything to get done. So I'm not usually shy, but suddenly the idea of walking up to the house next door and introducing myself to these strangers seemed a bit daunting. I decide to go for a bit of a skate first, just to get into the right frame of mind.

I sat down on the footpath to put my rollerblades on. A gang of kids were playing football on the green, and some younger kids were cycling around on bikes and tricycles. Woodland Green is a pretty nice place to live, I have to admit. It's nice to have lots of kids around and a place to hang out where our parents aren't freaking out about us getting knocked down or something. Just a pity for me that the only girl my age is

Ruby and her schedule is so busy we don't get as much hang-out time as we'd like. Well, there's also Tracey, but I don't count her. Tracey is the meanest girl I have ever met in my life. Her favourite thing to do is laugh at other people. She makes an actual hobby out of it. Unfortunately for me, she lives just two doors down from me, on the other side of the rented house. Just my luck that the nearest one of my classmates has to be meanie beanie Tracey.

I set off skating around the green, dodging out of the way of the little kids. It would be so nice to have someone new to hang out with. And having her right next door – what could be better? It would be somewhere to escape to when I'd had enough of my crazy family. I deliberately skated over and back in front of my own house and next door's. I was kind of hoping the new girl would see me, and she'd just come out herself, saving me the trouble of having to go and knock and introduce myself to her mum and all that.

'All OK there, Hannah?' It was Mum calling from the front door, Emma balanced on her hip.

'Yes. Fine,' I shouted back, hoping she'd just go away.

'Isn't there anyone home?' she roared.

'I don't know! I'm just going to see,' I hissed back, glancing around to see if anyone was watching.

Luckily shouts from inside our house told Mum that there was a fight that needed to be broken up, and she rushed off. I decided

I'd really better just get it over and done with before she came out again. Building up speed, I went up the path once more, then whizzed around and back down, not slowing down as I turned the corner into next door's driveway. Suddenly their house was rushing up to meet me. I put out my hands to stop myself from crashing into their front door. At that exact second the door started to open and I fell headlong into their hallway.

Chapter Two

'OW!' I didn't know which bit of me hurt most. It was a close contest between my wrist, which had bent awkwardly as I tried to break my fall, my left knee, which had taken most of my weight when it hit the wooden floor in the hallway, or my right shin, which I had whacked on the step as I fell. So much for all my safety gear, I thought.

'Is that how you always come into people's houses?'

I looked up to see the girl next door grinning down at me. 'I was just going to come out and see if you wanted to skate together, but now I think maybe you're a bit of a lia-bility.'

'It's not funny,' I muttered, rubbing my knee underneath my knee pad, which might have saved me from breaking any bones, but definitely hadn't stopped it from hurting. 'What did you go and open the door like that for?'

'Sorry,' she said, not sounding like she meant it a bit. 'I wasn't exactly expecting you to come crashing through it.'

I sat back and looked up at her properly. She had long blonde hair hanging loose down her back. She was wearing skinny jeans and a long T-shirt that said 'MEH' in really big letters. She smiled at me sud-denly, and her smile lit up her whole face. I couldn't help smiling back.

'I'm Hannah,' I told her, getting to my feet, or rather my blades. 'Sorry about that. It wasn't exactly how I was planning to introduce myself.'

'That's OK,' she said. 'I'm Meg. So, do you want to go skating together, or do you need to take a break?'

I was feeling slightly bruised, but I didn't want to admit it. 'I'm fine. Do you have roller-blades, then?'

'Yes, but I'm not exactly sure where. Do you want to come in for a minute while I look?'

'Sure.'

I followed her down the hall. It's always funny to see our house in reverse. From the outside Meg's and my house looked exactly the same, only the opposite way around.

Our sitting room window was on the right of the front door and that bit of the house joined on to Meg's, and the garage was on the left. Meg's sitting room window was on the left and the garage was on the right. The fronts of the houses were like mirror images of each other.

The insides were completely different though. Meg's house was painted cream all over – no, not cream – what's that really sensible plain colour rented houses always are? Oh yes, magnolia of course. The walls were bare, and the rooms seemed so empty, apart from all the boxes I mean – there were no books on the shelves yet, or ornaments on the mantelpiece, or anything that made it look like it actually belonged to them.

Meg led the way into the family room

at the back of the house. Almost the entire floor space was taken up with boxes and bags.

'I think I know what box they're in,' Meg said. 'Mum didn't want me to bring them because they're so bulky and take up so much space, but I knew I'd use them so I talked her into it.' She ripped the tape from the top of a box and peered inside. 'Huh – all her tennis stuff! She had room for that all right!' She held up two tennis rackets and a big sports bag, dumped them on the floor and dived into the box again. 'All her shoes too. And she thinks I have too many!' Several pairs of high heels came flying out to land on top of the tennis gear on the floor.

I was trying to work out her accent as she talked. She was Irish all right, but there was a hint of something else there too, I just couldn't figure it out.

'Aha!' Meg lifted out her rollerblades with a triumphant grin. 'I knew they were here somewhere. And here are all my knee pads and elbow pads and things. Mum insists on me wearing them – I suppose yours is the same?'

'Oh, yeah,' I said. 'She's very big on knee pads, elbow pads, helmets, seatbelts – all that stuff. I think it's some kind of a mum law that they have to be obsessed with safety.'

Meg was sitting on the floor pulling on her rollerblades. I suddenly realised how quiet the house was. 'Where is your mum, anyway?'

'Oh, she's gone out for the day. I've got the house to myself. It was starting to feel just a teeny bit too quiet, actually.'

'Oh my God, you're so lucky!' I told her. 'My house has never been quiet for a minute, ever. I can't actually imagine what it would be like to be the only one at home.'

'Really?'

I explained about all my siblings. Meg's eyes widened.

'Wow, you're the lucky one!' she said. 'I'm an only child. I always wished I had at least one sister to play with.'

I felt a bit bad. I knew I was lucky, really. 'Oh, I do like having a big family,' I said quickly. 'But sometimes I feel like I'd do anything to get five minutes' peace. I even have to come out to the front garden if I want to read my book because the boys have turned the back garden into a football pitch.'

Meg finished putting on all her gear, and we skated slowly to the front door. Normally Mum doesn't let me wear my rollerblades inside. But there were no grown-ups around to warn us about the wooden floor getting marked, so I glided along, enjoying the smooth feel of it underneath the blades.

We skated down the drive and started doing slow laps of the green. It was a bit quieter now – must have been snack time for the little kids – so it was easier to get around.

'So where did you used to live?' I asked her.

'Oh, we move around a lot,' Meg said vaguely. 'How about you – have you always lived in Carrickbeg?'

'Yes, my whole life,' I said. 'And your house has always been rented out, so we've had tons of different neighbours. The last lot were a big group of students, and they were really noisy. Mum was so glad when they moved.'

'Well, she needn't worry about us!' Meg said. 'It's just me and Mum, and we're pretty quiet.'

'What made you move to Carrickbeg?'

'Mum grew up here. She moved away when she went to college. My granny and grandad still live here, so Mum wanted to be near them when, um ...' She hesitated, then quickly said, 'when she decided to move. We used to come here a lot for holidays, but it's a few years now since we've been back.'

'So is Meg short for Megan then?' I asked her.

Meg made a face. 'I wish! My real name is Margaret, after my aunt. But if you EVER tell anyone ...'

I laughed. 'I won't! Meg is much nicer. Makes me think of Little Women.'

'Oh, I love Little Women!' Meg said. 'Although I think I like Amy better than Meg. I always think Amy is a bit more real – Meg's just too good to be true sometimes!'

'Laura's favourite is Jo,' I said. 'She wants to be a writer some day, so she just loves reading about Jo and how she keeps on writing stories and trying to get them published. Laura's one of my best friends,' I added in explanation.

'Does she live on the green too?' Meg asked.

'No, she's a bit further away. Ruby lives just over there,' I added, pointing to Ruby's house about ten doors down from Meg's, and on a bend so that it was facing the green from a different angle. 'But we can't call for her.' I explained about ballet camp.

'Are you going to any camps?' Meg asked.

'No.' I sighed. 'I'd have loved to go to drama.'

'Oh, do you like acting?'

'I love it. It's my favourite thing in school – I just wish we could do it more often. Did you do much in your old school?'

'A bit. I love it too,' Meg said. 'That feeling of transforming yourself into someone else, getting right inside their mind and the way they speak and move.'

'Exactly!' I beamed at her. It was so great to meet someone who understood just how I felt about acting.

By the time we'd circled the green a few times I'd told Meg all about my closest friends, Laura and Ruby, my crazy family and how I was dreading having to spend the summer holidays being an unpaid babysitter to my siblings. I kind of realised after a while that I'd been doing most of the talking, though. It wasn't that Meg was quiet, more that she kept asking questions about me, and she didn't volunteer very much information about herself. She didn't mention her dad, and she didn't seem to want to talk about why she and her mum had moved to Carrickbeg.

'Hannah!' It was Mum calling. 'I need you!'

'I'll only be a minute,' I told Meg. I was surprised Mum had actually remembered that she'd promised to call me in in case I needed to escape.

'It's OK, Mum,' I told her as I reached the door. 'Meg's really nice, I don't need you to call me in.'

'What? Oh, that's good,' Mum said, 'but actually, I need you anyway, I'm afraid. I've just remembered the boys are supposed to be going to a birthday party, and I've just put Emma down for a nap. Can you mind her and Maisie while I bring the boys?'

I called to Meg and started taking off my rollerblades as I explained to her that big sister duty was calling again. 'How about we meet up later? We can call for Ruby too.'

'Great! Let's do that.'

I watched as Meg skated back to her own house. Then Maisie called me to come and play teddies.

Not teddies again! I thought to myself, trying to suppress a sigh.

The morning had turned out better than

I had been expecting, and I felt pretty sure I had made a new friend in Meg. Maybe she could help me with my summer project – whatever it turned out to be. One thing was for sure, I needed to come up with something fast, or this babysitting thing could turn into a full-time job.

Chapter Three

All the time I was minding the girls, my mind was busily working away on a plan. Mum called me right after she dropped the boys at the party and said since she was out anyway she might as well go to Tesco, and did I mind looking after the girls for a bit longer? I said I didn't mind and she could go ahead. It was true, I didn't mind, not really. Being the oldest in the family does mean you have to help out sometimes, and I do actually like playing with Maisie and looking after Emma. I just didn't want the whole holidays to go by without me having done anything except play teddies, find lost soothers and break up rows. That would make a pretty boring 'What I did in my holidays' essay when I went back to school.

I kept thinking of Meg, all alone next door. It must be strange to move somewhere new and leave all your friends behind. I've lived in Carrickbeg all my life and I can't really imagine what it would be like if Mum and Dad suddenly announced we were moving to a new town. I'd miss Ruby and Laura so much and all the things we do together. I wondered if Meg was missing her friends and her old life.

Unbelievably, Maisie was tired of teddies. 'Will you read to me?' she asked.

'OK,' I agreed. 'Go and get your Secret Seven book.' We were working our way through the Secret Seven series together. I'd really enjoyed those books when I was a bit younger, and now it was nice to get a chance to read them again and see Maisie enjoying them too.

It was when we were curled up together reading about the adventures of Peter, Janet and all the rest that my super, brilliant, fantastic idea came to me. We should form a club! We'd need a clubhouse of some kind, and a secret password, and ways to get messages to each other. We'd each have our own job to do, and we'd hold regular meetings, and keep records in a secret journal.

'Han – nah!' Maisie was using her whiniest voice. I realised I'd stopped reading.

'Sorry, Maisie! I was just daydreaming there for a minute,' I told her. 'Why don't you read a little bit now, and I'll listen? I'll help you if you get stuck.'

Maisie took the book and started reading. My mind wandered off again. What would we do in the club, though? I was old enough to realise that the type of mysteries that the Secret Seven and the Five Findouters were always solving didn't really crop up like that all the time in real life. I wasn't sure I was cut out for life as a detective, anyway. Sitting in a café spying on people might be fun, but I wasn't so keen on the idea of snooping round old cottages in the dead of night, or trying to stay hidden while following someone on a bike, or having to dress up as a tramp to listen in on secret conversations.

Then I thought about wanting to go to drama camp. Was there some way I could put the ideas together? We wouldn't have a teacher, of course, or even a big group, but was there something we could do on our own?

'HANNAH!' Maisie was stuck on a word and I hadn't noticed.

'OK, Maisie, show me where you've got to,' I told her. I'd just have to work out the details later. But I felt the surge of happiness that having a new plan always brings.

As soon as Mum got home I hopped over the garden wall to knock on Meg's front door.

'Sorry to interrupt,' I said to Meg. 'I was just wondering if you can come over this after-noon?'

'Sure,' she said. 'What have you got in mind?'

'I'll explain everything later. Come over to my house about 2.30, OK?'

'See you then!' Meg said, smiling as she closed the door.

Now I just needed to get hold of the other two. I looked at my watch. Still only one o'clock, so I couldn't call over for Ruby just yet. I could drop a note in for her though, so she'd see it as soon as she got home from ballet camp. I'd have to call Laura from the landline at home. Ruby and I reckon we are the only twelve-year-olds in the entire country who don't have mobile phones. Mum says I don't need one until I go to secondary school next year. Laura has one, but she says it's not much use when she can't text her two best friends.

I just had time to phone Laura and tell her about the plan, then I rushed to help Mum unpack the groceries and make the lunch. The boys were getting a lift home from the party, so at least she didn't have to worry about that.

Mum said it was fine if I asked the girls over that afternoon, and she promised to keep Maisie occupied if I wanted to use my room. I wasn't so sure about that one. Keeping Maisie occupied is not easy, especially when you have three other children to look after too. I decided the garden was the best option, unless it started raining or something.

At quarter past two, I dragged the garden table into the middle of the lawn. Actually, that's where it's supposed to live, but the boys keep moving it because it gets in the way of their games. I set up four chairs and got a cloth to wipe away all the cobwebs –

it had been a while since we used it, and it looked like the spiders had taken it over. I got out my notebook and pen, and I filled a jug with juice and put it on a tray with four glasses.

The doorbell rang and I rushed to answer it.

'Hey,' said Ruby. 'I got your note – hope you don't mind me being early!'

'No, it's great! Come on in – you can help me with the biscuits and stuff.'

Ruby followed me in, saying hello to Mum and Emma as she passed. I've known Ruby since we were three years old. Our mothers met at toddler group. I'm maybe not as close to her as I am to Laura, but that's not because we don't get on or anything. It's really just because Ruby spends so much of her time on her ballet. As well as the normal classes she gets extra one-on-one lessons from the head of the ballet school, and she seems to spend most of the school holidays at a ballet camp. When she has a show coming up she has all these extra rehearsals, and she's forever doing exercises or stretches or something at home too. Ballet is the number one thing in her life, and Laura and I and her other friends are always going to come second to that. We don't mind though. We're really proud of Ruby, and when she is free to hang out with us, she's great fun.

Laura is super-talented too. Like I explained to Meg, she wants to be a writer when she grows up. Actually, she's a writer already, just not a published one yet. She goes through these dreamy phases when she's starting a new story, and gets completely caught up in the world of her characters. The rest of the time though, she's pretty normal, and she doesn't let it take over her life in quite the same way as Ruby's ballet does.

I don't have a special talent like my two best friends. Sometimes I wonder, if I got the right training and practised really really hard, if I could be good at drama. When I read a book or see a film that I love, I sometimes imagine myself playing that part, and what it would be like to be on the stage.

Ruby had just finished emptying a packet of biscuits onto a plate when the doorbell rang again. I was glad to see it was Laura – I wanted to tell them both about Meg before she got here.

'Hey, come on in! We're just waiting for Meg, then we've got the full group,' I told her.

'Oh, who's Meg?' Laura asked.

'She just moved in next door. I only met her this morning, but she's really nice.' I watched Laura's face carefully. When we were younger, she used to be a bit jealous if she thought I was making new friends without her. She'd kind of grown out of that, but I still felt a bit nervous. I didn't want her deciding she didn't like Meg before she'd even met her.

I needn't have worried, though. 'Oh, that's great,' Laura said. 'Remember you were worried it would be more screaming brats moving in next door!'

In the kitchen, Bobby was showing Ruby his latest kick-boxing move.

'Look, Ruby, you stand here,' he instructed her. 'Now watch.'

He took a couple of steps back, then screeched, 'Hi – YA!' and came running towards her, jumping and kicking his leg in the air at the same time.

Ruby screamed and then giggled. 'Wow, Bobby. You're getting really good at that.'

'Why don't you show Zach?' I suggested.

'But I want to show Ruby what comes next,' Bobby said.

'Another time maybe. I need Ruby now,' I told him.

'OK,' Bobby sighed. He went running off, shouting to Zach to come and practise with him.

'Quick, let's go outside before they come back,' I said.

I picked up the tray and Ruby opened the patio door so I could carry it out to the back garden. I liked being the host – it made me feel very grown-up.

We settled down at the table.

'So what's this big plan you mentioned?' Ruby wanted to know. 'It sounded really mysterious in your note.'

'Yeah, I'm dying to know too. Your plans are always either completely brilliant, or else they land us in a lot of trouble,' Laura said with a laugh.

'Like the time you decided we should have a yard sale to surprise our parents, only you sold a whole lot of things you weren't supposed to,' Ruby giggled.

'Like your dad's favourite tie,' Laura said. 'And your mum's sunglasses.'

'And a cake tin belonging to your granny,' Ruby said.

'And the book my mum was in the middle of reading,' Laura added.

'The book was your idea!' I pointed out. I pretended to be cross. 'Fine, if you don't want to hear my brilliant plan, I won't tell you.'

'Of course we do,' Laura said in a soothing tone. 'We'll just be a bit better prepared this time, and put all our valuables in a safe place.'

'Please tell us, I'm dying to hear now!' Ruby said.

'I'll tell you everything when Meg gets here,' I promised. 'Actually, it's only the start of a plan. I need you guys to help me turn it into a proper one.'

'Hey.' It was Meg, peeping over the hedge between our two gardens, and looking a little shy.

'Hi, Meg! Have you found the secret passage in our garden?'

It wasn't really a secret passage, but I was still in an Enid Blyton kind of mood. I showed her the gap in the hedge where she could squeeze through. It's my favourite sneaky hiding place when I'm playing hide and seek with my brothers.

'This is great!' Meg said, emerging from the hedge into our garden. 'So much handier than going all the way round to the front door.'

I brought her over to the table where the others were looking at her curiously, Laura shading her eyes from the sun with her hand.

'This is Ruby, and this is Laura,' I said.

'Guys, this is Meg.'

'Hi,' they all said.

'Meg just moved in next door,' I explained.

'Are your parents busy unpacking?' Ruby said.

'Oh, it's just me and Mum,' Meg said.

'My parents are separated too,' Laura told her. 'It sucks at first, but you kind of get used to it.'

A funny look crossed Meg's face. I had already worked out that she wasn't ready to talk about whatever was going on in her family, so I thought I'd better change the subject.

'So I wanted you all to come over because I've got this idea,' I said. 'I think we should form a club.'

I sat back, waiting for them all to exclaim

in delight at the idea.

No one said anything.

'What kind of a club?' Laura asked at last.

'This isn't going to be one of your Secret Seven type ideas again, is it?' Ruby said, sounding sceptical.

I remembered then that I'd tried to set up a club with Ruby and Laura ages ago. It was supposed to be like the Secret Seven, but as there were only three of us I christened us the Terrific Three. We made membership badges and drew up a club code, and we had to use a secret password to get into each other's bedrooms. The idea kind of fizzled out when we realised there just weren't any mysteries out there which we could solve. Well, not unless you count the mystery of who had stolen Laura's Easter egg, and we already knew that the answer to that was her big sister Andrea, except we couldn't prove it because she'd eaten the evidence.

'Of course not,' I said, trying to sound as dignified as possible. 'We were only little kids then. This is something different. We'd have regular meetings, and we'd all have different jobs in the club. It would be kind of like a summer project, only a fun one, not like you have in school, and our parents would have to let us meet up with each other because it would be club business.'

'I like that idea,' Ruby said slowly. 'I mean, ballet camp is going to take up a lot of my time, so if I want to see you guys it would be good to have something I need to go to so Mum doesn't say "oh, not now", or "maybe after dinner" or whatever.'

'Yes, but ...' said Laura, '... you still haven't said what we're actually going to DO.'

'Well, here's the thing,' I said. I was almost afraid to say the next part in case they didn't like it. 'You know the way I was really hoping to go to drama camp ... well, I just thought, why don't we have a sort of drama camp of our own? Ruby, you know all about being on the stage because of your ballet, and Laura, you're really good at writing, so you could help us come up with scripts and things like that. And Meg likes acting too, so we've got everything we need.'

I stopped talking and looked around to see everyone's reaction.

'I think it's a great idea!' Meg said. 'We could have rehearsals and plan a show. Laura could write something for us, or we could just adapt a story we know, like a fairytale or something.'

I smiled at her in relief and looked at the other two. They were smiling too – phew!

'Brilliant,' Laura said.

'I love it,' Ruby said.

I couldn't help bouncing up and down in my chair. 'Yay! I can't wait to get started!'

BOOK IN
FOR YOUR NEW ADVENTURE TODAY

CELEBRATING

WORLD
BOOK
DAY

20

2 MARCH 2017

3 brilliant ways to continue YOUR reading adventur

1 VISIT YOUR LOCAL BOOKSHOP

Your go-to destination for awesome reading recommendations and events with your favourite authors and illustrators.

 Booksellers.org.uk/bookshopsearch

2 JOIN YOUR LOCAL LIBRARY

Browse and borrow from a huge selection of books, get expert ideas of what to read next, and take part in wonderful family reading activities – all for FREE!

FIND YOUR LOCAL LIBRARY Findalibrary.co.uk

3 DISCOVER A WORLD OF STORIES ONLINE

32 podcasts to try

Stuck for ideas of what to read next? Plug yourself in to our brilliant new podcast library! Sample a world of amazing books, brought to life by amazing storytellers. worldbookday.com

SPONSORED

NATION
BOO
toker

HAPPY BIRTHDAY WORLD BOOK DAY!

Let's celebrate . . .

Can you believe this year is our **20th birthday** – and thanks to you, as well as our amazing authors, illustrators, booksellers, librarians and teachers, there's SO much to celebrate!

Did you know that since WORLD BOOK DAY began in 1997, we've given away over **275 million book tokens**? WOW! We're delighted to have brought so many books directly into the hands of millions of children and young people just like you, with a gigantic assortment of fun activities and events and resources and quizzes and dressing-up and games too – we've even broken a **Guinness World Record**!

Whether you love discovering books that make you **laugh**, CRY, *hide under the covers* or **drive your imagination wild**, with WORLD BOOK DAY, there's always something for everyone to choose–as well as ideas for exciting new books to try at bookshops, libraries and schools everywhere.

And as a small charity, we couldn't do it without a lot of help from our friends in the publishing industry and our brilliant sponsor, NATIONAL BOOK TOKENS. Hip-hip hooray to them and three cheers to you, our readers and everyone else who has joined us over the last 20 years to make WORLD BOOK DAY happen.

Happy Birthday to us – and happy reading to you!

SPONSORED BY

#WorldBookDay20